He's Crazy but Cute!

It's all here! Learn about your favorite Hanson brother, Zachary Walker Hanson!

★ Does he mind being the youngest member of the group?
★ How did he choose to play the drums?
★ Is he *ever* serious?
★ Could YOU be the perfect girl for him?

Find all these answers and more in . . .

Zac Hanson: Totally Zac!

Look for other biographies from Archway Paperbacks

CELEBRITY

Hanson: MMMBop to the Top by Jill Matthews
Isaac Hanson: Totally Ike! by Nancy Krulik
Taylor Hanson: Totally Taylor! by Nancy Krulik
Zac Hanson: Totally Zac! by Matt Netter
Jonathan Taylor Thomas: Totally JTT! by Michael-Anne Johns
Prince William: The Boy Who Will Be King by Randi Reisfeld
Will Power!: A Biography of Will Smith by Jan Berenson

SPORTS

Grant Hill: A Biography
Michael Jordan: A Biography
Shaquille O'Neal: A Biography
Tiger Woods: A Biography
  by Bill Gutman
Skating for the Gold: Michelle Kwan & Tara Lipinski
  by Chip Lovitt

INSPIRATIONAL

**Warriors Don't Cry: A Searing Memoir of the Battle to Integrate
  Little Rock's Central High** by Melba Pattillo Beals
**To the Stars: The Autobiography of George Takei, Star Trek's Mr.
  Sulu** by George Takei

zac hanson

TOTALLY ZAC!
an unauthorized biography

matt netter

AN ARCHWAY PAPERBACK
Published by POCKET BOOKS
New York   London   Toronto   Sydney   Tokyo   Singapore

AN ARCHWAY PAPERBACK *Original*

An Archway Paperback published by
POCKET BOOKS, a division of Simon & Schuster Inc.
1230 Avenue of the Americas, New York, NY 10020

ISBN: 0-671-02445-0

First Archway Paperback printing February 1998

10 9 8 7 6 5 4 3

AN ARCHWAY PAPERBACK and colophon are registered trademarks of Simon & Schuster Inc.

Front cover photo by David Tonge/Retna

Printed in the U.S.A.

IL 4+

Special thanks to Jane Ginsberg, Lisa Clancy,
Liz Shiflett, and, especially, Karen Lynne
for all their support

CONTENTS

INTRODUCTION

Picture the cutest guy in your school, the one you and your friends can't stop passing notes about. Think of the class clown, the one whose outrageous behavior puts everyone in stitches. Lastly, picture the most talented kid in school—the athlete, artist, or musician—the one who makes you green with envy. Now combine all three in one and make them a celebrity on top of it. That's Zachary Hanson, a preteen dream!

As the youngest member of pop music's hottest band, Zac qualifies as one of the most famous and successful kids in the world. In many ways, Zac is a typical twelve-year-old boy—wide-eyed, fearless, and brimming with energy. However, after an all-American upbringing in Tulsa, Oklahoma, Zachary has seen his life suddenly become anything but ordinary. In a whirlwind year, he and his brothers Isaac and Taylor's lofty ambitions were suddenly realized beyond their wildest dreams. From humble beginnings, Hanson is now a chart-topping, heart-stopping, "MMMBopping" sensation, the likes of which haven't been seen since the Beatles in the '60s!

Introduction

Like a tornado, Hanson whirled through America in the spring of '97, winning young hearts over and gaining adult respect at every turn. In an all-out media blitz, the Hanson brothers presented themselves as the stars of tomorrow. By early summer, "MMMBop" brought feel-good music back to the radio. And through a series of summer TV appearances and promotional concerts, the brothers spread a wave of Hanson fever that would reach epidemic proportions. Isaac, Taylor, and Zachary traveled the world over, and Hansonmania followed them at every stop. At the very core of this growing sensation is a singing, songwriting, crowd-pleasing, drumming dynamo ... who plays Sega and goes trick-or-treating.

How does twelve-year-old Zac handle the rigors of practice, performance, interviews, photo shoots, travel, being away from home, and, of course, all the attention from fans while he's in sixth grade? Can he still find time for family and friends, homework, or even sleep? How could a kid be a professional drummer? How can three brothers spend that much time together and not kill each other? What are Zac's interests and hobbies? What's he really like? Does Zac have a girlfriend? If not, would he date a fan? You'll find the answers to all of these questions and get the scoop on some of the zaniest things Zac's ever said and done. Where's the love? Turn the page and start reading!

zac hanson

ZAC ATTACK!

If Hanson were an automobile, Taylor would be the ignition, Isaac would be the steering wheel, and Zac would have a dual role, as both the accelerator and the horn! Make way for Zac, the wackiest, most hyper member of Hanson and the youngest drummer in rock-and-roll.

It's incredible to think that there's a professional musician who plays with Power Rangers. This couldn't be more appropriate, as Zac himself is very much a superhero with a whole utility belt full of endearing tricks. If his high-octane drumming doesn't blow you away, his winning smile will. If Zac's crazy antics don't get you laughing, his knee-jerk wisecracks will. If the advanced level of his

1

musical talent isn't enough to impress you, then surely his wise-beyond-his-years knowledge will. And if his charm isn't enough to melt your heart, his dreamy, pinup-worthy face will set it afire!

What immediately comes to mind when any Hanson fan thinks of Zac is his outrageous behavior. Whether it's onstage, in the studio, or at home, you can bet Zac will be the center of attention. "I'm goofy stupid," Zac says in an attempt to describe his nature. Like any younger brother, Zac always finds a new way to annoy his brothers. Whether it's jumping on Isaac's back during an interview or making faces at Taylor during a photo shoot, he always knows just how to push their buttons. Ike and Tay usually just laugh it off, though, as it provides good comic relief for the young trio, who still get nervous before big events and often miss home while they're on the road.

THE TRULY UNIQUE ONE

Often called "a young Jim Carrey," "the class clown of the band," and "hyper drive," Zac's one nickname that has stuck is the one his brothers gave him. "Animal" is what Isaac and Taylor playfully call him, after the wild-haired, rambunctious drummer on *The Muppet Show*. The name fits because Zac certainly

2

is animated. "I always have to be wacky," Zac explains. "When I act serious, it's like, 'Why aren't you wacky? Is this a bad day for you?'"

Everywhere the Hanson brothers have gone, Zac's reputation has been upheld. There's not one reporter who's ever interviewed the band who didn't get a firsthand taste of Zac's quick wit. During an interview with MTV, Zac got impatient when the reporter directed the first three or four questions at Isaac and Taylor. "You know, *I'm* not talking here!" he reminded them. Moments later, Zac pretended to fall asleep.

Likewise, there's not one photographer who's ever shot Hanson who didn't witness Zac's explosive energy. During photo shoots, it's hard to get Zac to stay still. If he's not clowning around, he's running full speed through the corridors of the office, as he did during Hanson's scheduled shoot with *16* magazine. If you've ever owned a kitten, you can begin to understand Zac's energy level.

In a sense, Zac's hyperactivity is his biggest strength. It's part of what makes him such a good drummer and all of what makes him so much fun to watch during a performance. Surely, fans applaud Hanson because of their great harmonies and bouncy beats. But it's Zac who encourages the crowd to turn it up a notch. The enthusiastic clapping and cheering quickly turn to ground-shaking stomping and ear-piercing shrills after Zac gets the fans fired up. You never know to what lengths Zac will go to accomplish this until he does it. He might scream, "Louder!" at the first sign of applause, as he did at Hanson's mini-gig outside the *Today* show studio in New York City's Rockefeller Center. He might leap over a dividing rail into the crowd, as he pretended to do at a performance outside the Sam Goody at Universal City Walk in California. He might even do something really spontaneous and pull a lucky fan onstage, as he did during one of Hanson's early Tulsa-area concerts.

THE SERIOUS SIDE OF ZAC

What you can never lose sight of, however, is that when it comes to his music, Zachary is all business. Zac's been around music his whole life. His parents sang to him as a baby, and by the time he was six, he began singing himself. It didn't take long for his family to realize that Zac had the same love of music that his older brothers had. When the three boys sang together at the dinner table one night, the whole family took notice of the magic they'd uncovered. This special harmony that the young boys created would lay the foundation for the incredible stardom that Hanson has now attained.

In the years that followed, Zac and his brothers grew as musicians as they matured into young men. Parents Walker and Diana realized that their sons were serious about making music. Playing old hand-me-down instruments, Isaac, Taylor, and Zachary went from school to school playing at gymnasiums and small auditoriums. Before long, the schools became town fairs and then local clubs. They shopped their homemade CD to record companies, and after a long while, a lot of hard work, and one lucky break, all their passion and determination paid off and they got a record deal. Now they sell out huge arenas and have a CD that's six times platinum (that's six million copies sold).

Zac enjoys every minute of his band's success, but he never loses sight of what it took them to get to where they are today. He appreciates every aspect of Hanson's career, no matter how exhausting the flights may be or how grueling the schedule may seem. Perhaps that is why Zac seems to live for the moment.

SHORT BUT IMPORTANT

Never underestimate the importance of Zachary to Hanson. He is so much more than just a drummer. Zac is a singer, and not just a backup singer. Zac sings lead on four different Hanson songs, parts of several others, and backup on all the rest. Zac is also a songwriter. He has every bit as much to do with the writing of lyrics and the composing of music as his older brothers do. Zac's input on their recordings, performances, and even videos is taken on the same level. As far as his drumming is concerned, Zac is not just good for his age. He is a truly talented drummer who keeps a beat, maintains a steady rhythm, and can even solo. If he's this good at twelve, there's no telling how fantastic he can be when he's twenty-five or thirty.

Interesting fact: if Zachary Hanson were all of one month younger, he would have broken the record for the youngest musician ever to record a number one song. When Hanson's "MMMBop" reached number one, Zac was just eleven years and six months old. Michael Jackson, then the youngest member of his brotherly band the Jackson Five, was eleven years and five months old when their single "I Want You Back" topped the charts.

WHAT'S HE LIKE, ANYWAY?

Zac grew up in a suburban neighborhood, part of a big family. In addition to himself, Isaac, and Taylor, there are two younger sisters and a younger brother. A new baby is expected in 1998. If you're counting, that makes seven. Zac is home-schooled and is the equivalent of a sixth-grader. He's a self-proclaimed whiz at math, and he's also a tremendous artist. In his free time, Zac designs his own comic books. He also loves his Sega Saturn and Sony PlayStation, plays soccer, and Rollerblades. But by far his favorite thing to do is "go to Laser Quest!"

Naturally, Zac spends a lot of hours practicing his drums. He hasn't gotten as good as he is by accident! In addition to practicing, recording, and performing with brothers Isaac and Taylor, Zac also has quite an ear for music. Like most kids and teens, Zac has a stereo and a Walkman that he likes to take with him on the road. His CD collection includes favorites like Boyz II Men, En Vogue, Aerosmith, the Spin Doctors, and Counting Crows, as well as some oldies but goodies like the Jackson Five, Aretha Franklin, and the Beatles.

Zac doesn't watch too much TV. Between his music career and schoolwork, there isn't much time. Plus, Zac is more of an outdoors person, opting for the backyard or playground over the living-room couch. He does admit to liking cartoons and is a big fan of *Animaniacs*. Zac goes for action movies over dramas and especially gets into big-budget, blockbuster special-effects flicks, like *Twister* and *Total Recall*. Zac loves fast food, especially McDonald's and a Tulsa favorite, Rex's Boneless Chicken. He especially loves dessert foods, however, such as Jell-O and chocolate ice cream.

You may have noticed that Zac likes clothes. He doesn't have a particular style, and he's not particularly trendy, but he loves to experiment with different materials, such as satin and velvet. He wears many different types of shirts, some striped, some solid, some earth tones, some bright colors. He generally goes for baggy pants and doesn't get into jewelry and accessories as much as his brother Tay does. The most important item of clothing to Zac is shoes. He takes tremendous pride in his vast collection of Doc Martens. Zac seems to have a pair in every color and style and went on a shopping spree at the Doc Martens factory outlet store while in London.

Zac loves his family and, in addition to his parents and two older brothers, he enjoys spending time with his little sisters, Jessica, nine, and Avery, six, and little bro Mackenzie, three. Zac also spends plenty of time with people his own age. When he gets together with his neighborhood pals, they usually skateboard and play basketball. Aside from being famous, Zac, in many ways, is just like any other kid his age.

GROWING UP HANSON

Diana and Walker Hanson welcomed their third child into the world on October 22, 1985. The angelic, fair-haired, and brown-eyed boy was christened Zachary Walker. Although the middle name is his father's, unlike his older brothers, Zachary would go by his first name. Family and friends have affectionately called him Zac since he was a baby.

Zac's parents brought him back to their semirural home in the affluent west side of Tulsa, Oklahoma. Awaiting tiny Zac's arrival were his brothers, Jordan Taylor, then three, and Clarke Isaac, then five, who'd been raised in the same home thus far. Diana and Walker had lived in Tulsa long before they had children or even met, for that matter. In fact,

10

they'd lived there their entire lives, as had their parents and grandparents before them.

Smack in the middle of the United States lies Tulsa, the second-largest city in Oklahoma. If you're from a big city like New York or Los Angeles, you may think of Tulsa as a laidback farm town. However, if you are from a small rural town in the Midwest or Deep South, you might say Tulsa is a fast-paced city. It's kind of both, actually, and that's what makes it a special place. Tulsa has 400,000 residents, a booming oil industry, and a downtown area rich with culture. On the other hand, Tulsa is divided by the Arkansas River and borders on rolling hills and fertile land.

Taking full advantage of Tulsa's beautiful landscape is the Hanson home, which features a generous property line. After all, with six kids in the family, a big backyard is essential. "We play basketball and football, we Rollerblade, and we have a soccer goal in our backyard," Zac says. "We have a tree house that we built in the backyard." There also had to be plenty of room for pets. "We once had six cats," Zac tells, "but that was because the mother gave birth to a litter of five."

SIBLING REVELRY

Zac describes his relationship with Isaac and Taylor as ideal. "We really don't fight," he says. "We get along very well. We're basically best friends." Sure, they had their occasional tiffs growing up; after all, boys will be boys. But, with loving parents and a strong faith, the Hanson brothers never held grudges. "What is there to argue about?" Zac wonders. "We've always been close."

Ike, Tay, and Zac have had a nontraditional education by some standards. They are home-schooled. Zac says "home-schooling is a big thing in Tulsa," and he doesn't understand why people find it strange. "Our mom wanted to home-school us because she wanted to have a better relationship with us," Zac explains. This doesn't mean Zac sits around and watches cartoons all day, although sometimes he'd like to. It just means that instead of riding the bus to a school building, the Hanson boys have tutors come to their home. Many classes, in fact, are taught by Mom herself. Talk about playing favorites! The advantage of home-schooling is that it makes for a more flexible schedule, which has been invaluable to their music careers. "I don't think we could be a band without home-schooling," Zac surmises.

Before the rigors of a musical career kept Zac so occupied, he always found time to play—when his homework was finished, of course. Although he considers his bros to be his best pals, Zac had plenty of neighborhood playmates as well. "We're kids that do stuff," Zac says. "There's a local place called Laser Quest. We go there a lot."

RAISED ON RADIO

Before Zac was old enough even to shake a rattle, much less conquer the enemy at Laser Quest, his family would sing lullabies to him. First Mom and Dad, then Isaac and Taylor, and, eventually, Zac would be old enough to chime in himself. Just as love, morals, and religion played important roles in Zac's upbringing, so did music.

When Zac was old enough to squawk, his father encouraged him to say "Amen" in unison with his brothers at the dinner table. Technically, this qualifies as Zachary's first attempt at harmony. Zac's mom, Diana, has always been a fan of Billy Joel. Ike and Tay remember singing his hit song "The Longest Time" together. At the tender age of three, Zac would listen and try to sing along with them.

Diana and Walker wanted music to have the same positive influence on their sons' lives that it had had on them. Diana majored in music as a college student. Walker has played guitar through much of his life. Together, they sang in the Horizons, a church choir group.

However, the Hanson parents never seriously considered performing as a career. Diana focused her attentions on motherhood and home-schooling. The Hanson home eventually would become the small schoolhouse it is today, as Isaac, Taylor, and Zachary were later joined by Jessica, Avery, and Mackenzie.

Meanwhile, dear old Dad, like many Oklahomans, works for an oil company. Walker quickly climbed the ranks of Helmerich & Payne until he was promoted to an international manager position. This would uproot the Hanson family from Tulsa, at least temporarily. On work assignment, Walker and his family would have to relocate to South America for a year, spending time in Ecuador, Venezuela, and Trinidad.

SOUTH AMERICAN SINGING

Since the boys were being home-schooled and Mom was their teacher, relocating wasn't a problem for the Hanson clan. They kept their Tulsa home with plans of returning to it after Walker's transfer assignments were completed. Zac and his brothers were instructed by their parents to pack only the bare essentials for the temporary move. Along with their toothbrushes and plenty of clean underwear, Isaac, Taylor, and Zachary packed a tape recorder and a series of "not sold in stores" Time/Life tapes that they'd had their parents order for them from a TV commercial. Since the places they'd be living in didn't offer cable TV and many of the other modern conveniences the boys were used to, Diana and Walker deemed the music essential as well. Diana thought it might also help remind the boys of home and help alleviate any homesickness. When they arrived in South America, Walker set up the tape player before the family even opened their suitcases.

During their time in South America and the Caribbean, Diana continued instructing the boys. Their lesson plan was a little different from what they'd grown used to, but in the end, the Hanson boys would learn about a new culture and a new people, in ways they never could from a textbook. There was no shortage of strange animals to observe, either! Their play time was a bit different as well. With warm weather most of the year, Zac and his brothers would get to enjoy afternoon swims in the tropical waters almost every day. When it rained, they had the tapes.

The Time/Life tapes featured popular rock-and-roll and R&B songs from the '50s and '60s. Musicians who paved the way for modern music, such as Bobby Darrin, Chuck Berry, Little Richard, Otis Redding, Aretha

Franklin, and early Beatles, delivered songs like "Rockin' Robin," "Splish Splash," and "Johnny B. Goode." "That is the best music," Zac says. The boys would end up listening to those tapes until they nearly wore out. By then, they knew all of them by heart and began singing along with them. These tapes would not only be a music lesson and a pastime but eventually would become a source of inspiration for the songs that Hanson would later write. In fact, to this day, all three Hanson brothers can still recite the lyrics, word for word, of every song on those tapes!

"The boys really started singing when we went overseas," Walker shared with one reporter. "At night, I would get the guitar and play for them for half an hour." And Isaac and Taylor would sing their little hearts out.

"We started doing two-part harmony," Isaac says.

"But the two-part harmony didn't really sound too right," interjects Zac. "So they needed a third person!" From this point forward, they sang as a trio.

The Hanson boys returned to the United States, and Tulsa, with new knowledge and fond memories of a special experience. Most significantly, they returned with a stronger appreciation of music and a love for singing.

FROM THE TOP

Upon their return home, the Hanson boys got back to the things they had missed, such as cable TV and American radio. But they still put aside plenty of time for their favorite pastime, singing. The more they sang, the more their harmony developed. As Ike got older and learned how to play the piano, the brothers began putting their own spin on some of the songs they liked to sing. They started singing them to their little sister, Jessica, and later, in 1991, to their new baby sister, Avery. Eventually, they wrote their own lyrics and came up with their own melodies for songs about their little siblings.

The boys became so passionate about playing music together that their chores would get neglected. Mom and Dad would go out to run an errand and ask that the dishes be done while they were gone. When they returned, the sink was still piled high with dirty dishes. It's not that Ike, Tay, and Zac were disrespectful or lazy. "Instead of doing our chores," Zac explains, "we usually spent the time writing a new song." Would Mom and Dad be mad? Not as Zac describes it. "They'd say, 'This better be good,' and give us a chance to sing it. Then, of course, we'd still have to do the dishes!" he adds.

SONGS OF THEIR OWN

Pretty soon, the boys began taking a more organized approach to their songwriting. As they thought of new lyrics, they would write them down rather than keeping them in their heads. Isaac began taking piano lessons, as would Taylor and Zac later on. The brothers started developing melodies all their own and putting them together with the lyrics they had written. Their first completed original song was called "Rain Falling Down." Isaac was in third grade at the time, and Zac was all of four years old.

For the next few years, Ike, Tay, and Zac would continue practicing, writing songs, and taking piano lessons. Although the boys had plenty of other friends in the Tulsa area, Zac says, "When we were younger, with our best friends, we'd always ask, 'Do you wanna be in a group?' But in the end, it was just us."

Up until 1991, the Hanson brothers had played only in the living room of their home, in front of family, friends, and neighbors. At the end of that year, Walker had an idea. He brought his sons to his office Christmas party. Without planning or warning, Isaac, Taylor, and Zachary, then eleven, eight, and six, got up and sang in front of hundreds of employees and their families. Snapping their fingers and singing a few '50s do-wop tunes, the boys soon had their surprised audience clapping along to their unrehearsed performance. "That really got their juices flowing," Walker explained to a local reporter.

When it became obvious that music was more than just a hobby to Isaac, Taylor, and Zachary, Walker and Diana provided support and guidance at every turn. "It was obvious we were serious," Zac explains. "They encouraged us with getting bookings and things like that."

In 1992, the Hanson brothers began performing in front of small crowds at family gatherings and parties. As word-of-mouth spread, they began playing at town functions and school gymnasiums. The three brothers would dress alike, and all had neatly combed short hair then. Since they only played piano, they sang a cappella (without instruments). They played covers of all those '50s and '60s songs they learned to love while in South America and the Caribbean and mixed in a few ditties of their own. They called themselves "The Hanson Brothers."

Since Diana and Walker Hanson both have musical backgrounds and their boys started so young, some people have suggested that the boys were pushed by their parents. To this, Zac jokingly responds, "Our parents forced us into this! Help us!" On a more serious note, Zac emphasizes, "Our parents are not *stage* parents. They're supportive. They're completely behind us, and they have always been.

"Without them, we couldn't drive to our shows!" Zac says with a giggle. More seriously, he adds, "Our parents didn't push us into this. They said, 'We're going to drive you where you want to go and get you what you need.'"

THE FIRST BIG GIGS

As they refined their act, the boys took dance lessons and incorporated the footwork into their act. Early Hanson performances were compared to New Edition. In May of 1992, the Hanson Brothers performed at Mayfest, an annual Tulsa festival. Zac recalls, "At that point, we were singing a cappella. We got started because we love singing and we love music."

The Hanson Brothers started playing at state fairs in other cities outside Tulsa, and with each performance, the Hansons won over more and more young fans. In all, Ike, Tay, and Zac performed more than two hundred shows and established a name for themselves. Diana began selling T-shirts at the shows, as well as getting the names and addresses of fans to start a mailing list. As word got out, more and more people began coming to see the young sensations perform. This gave Diana another idea. Why not put together a CD of all their music to sell to fans at shows?

That's exactly what they did. After compiling more than fifty of their own original songs over the past few years, plus developing their own spin on many R&B classics, they had more than enough material. Mom and Dad found a local studio and hired a few area musicians and producers to help out. By early 1995, the Hansons put their five best original songs ("Boomerang," "Don't Accuse," "Rain," "More Than Anything," and "More Than Anything—Reprise") together, with a few cover songs of groups like the Jackson Five, on a CD and entitled it *Boomerang*. They had a few thousand copies made that were sold at their shows and at local record stores and also submitted as demos to record companies.

LITTLE DRUMMER BOY

None of the record companies bit, but this didn't discourage Zac and his brothers in the least. Although Ike, Tay, and Zac had a great measure of respect for classic rock-and-roll and R&B, they began taking a liking to modern music as well. Listening to groups such as Counting Crows, 10,000 Maniacs, the Spin Doctors, Boyz II Men, Ace of Base, and even Aerosmith gave the boys some inspiration as well. They decided they wanted to add some instruments to their act.

Taylor had developed into the best piano player of the three, so he took the keyboards, and Ike always had an interest in guitar from his dad's influence. With his live-wire persona, Zac and the drums seemed to be a marriage

23

made in heaven. "I couldn't play guitar or piano, so that's how I went to the drums," Zac explains. "The secret is, nobody else's arms are as long. I couldn't play the guitar or piano, so I went to the drums because I've got long arms."

Taylor borrowed his first keyboards from a friend, and Ike got his guitar from a pawn shop. "A friend of ours had an old, used Ludwig drum set in the attic," Zac remembers. With no lessons, it didn't come easy for Zac and Ike. "In the beginning, we weren't very good at our instruments. We're pretty much self-taught, and when we started playing, we just did simple stuff. Bang, bang, bang!"

Regardless of how new at this they may have been, after just a week of practice, they got back onstage. The boys showed tremendous resolve, but their first few shows had their share of problems. "When we first started," Zac remembers, "these secondhand Ludwig drums that I had wouldn't stay still—they'd roll around the stage!"

Persistence paid off, because once Ike, Tay, and Zac all improved their instrument playing, they abandoned the dance routine and began focusing on making upbeat, fast-paced songs. Hanson's first true club gig soon followed at the Blue Rose Cafe, one of Tulsa's hottest places for bands to perform. The only hitch was that the club served alcohol, so the boys weren't allowed *inside!* Just the same, Hanson performed its set in the club's parking lot and attracted a huge crowd.

THE PATH TO STARDOM BEGINS HERE

By the time Ike, Tay, and Zac were proficient enough on their instruments and had written enough new songs to make another record, Zac was about ten and already a pretty darn good drummer. "I'm not that great a drummer," a modest Zac explains, "but everyone says I can play, so I'll take their word for it."

This time around, the songs on the CD would all be theirs. Instrument playing was now to be featured as prominently as the vocals. The sound on their second CD is so different from *Boomerang* that at times it doesn't even sound like the same group. The original tracks were short, upbeat pop songs with catchy melodies like the music many of their idols had made. But, as much of a Jackson Five feel as it had to it, it also had a modern spin with obvious influences from the groups the boys had been listening to more recently. Zac and his brothers named the album *MMMBop* after one of the songs on it.

MMMBop featured fifteen original Hanson songs, including "Thinking of You," "With You in Your Dreams," and two versions of "MMMBop," which would all wind up on *Middle of Nowhere.* The rest of the songs were "Day Has Come," "Two Tears," "Stories," "River," "Surely As the Sun," "Something New," "Soldier," "Pictures," "Incredible," "Sometimes," and "Baby You're So Fine." As if twelve Hanson songs you've never heard isn't enough to make you want to get your hands on a rare copy of this album, here's another enticing factoid. The inside cover of the CD features original artwork done by Ike, Tay, and Zac. They drew funny faces, dinosaurs, a drum set, and other weird stuff. Unfortunately, the odds of anyone outside Tulsa ever finding a copy of *MMMBop* are about the same as winning the lottery. For the sake of Hanson fans everywhere, let's hope *MMMBop* is rereleased in some format, someday.

While putting *MMMBop* together, the Hanson family took a trip to Austin, Texas, for the South by Southwest Music Conference, a place where record industry executives come in search of new talent. The Hanson brothers, who'd now started going by the name "Hanson," walked around asking people if they could sing for them. By chance, one person who obliged was then Dave Mathews Band manager Christopher Sabec. Sabec was so impressed that he said to the boys, "Where are your parents? I need to speak to them."

Months later, after *MMMBop* was completed, Sabec stopped by the Hanson home and talked to the boys and their parents about a musical career. Ike, Tay, and Zac—and the whole family, for that matter—felt very comfortable with Sabec, and after he wound up staying with them for more than a week, Hanson made him its manager.

A lot of Sabec's friends and colleagues in the record industry warned him that he might be making a mistake taking on a young, unpolished act like Hanson. After all, two and three years ago, record companies weren't looking for the next Jackson Five, they wanted the next Nirvana. The Seattle alternative music scene, as well as the Los Angeles hard-core rap scene, had exploded in the early '90s, leaving little room for a young, feel-good pop group. "I think everybody's tired of being sad," Zac points out. "There's still alternative music, but some people want to listen to music that isn't so 'I hate life.'"

Sabec was confident that Zac was right. Pop music was about to make a comeback, and

Sabec saw it coming. Other record companies weren't quite so sure yet. Sabec sent copies of *MMMBop* to several record companies. But it wasn't until the disc landed on the desk of Steve Greenberg at Mercury Records that things started happening.

MAN FROM MERCURY

MMMBop was finally in the right hands, but for Hanson, that was just the beginning. After giving the CD a listen, Greenberg's initial reaction was that it was a fake. He didn't believe that three kids could possibly have written and performed those songs by themselves. "I loved it, but I was sure there was some adult pulling the strings, or the vocals were manipulated, and they weren't really playing their instruments," Greenberg explains.

In June of 1996, Sabec invited Greenberg to Coffeyville, Kansas, where Hanson was to perform at a county fair, to prove to him that they were the real deal. "They played great, they sang great," Greenberg recalls. "There wasn't an adult in sight, except their dad, who was loading up the equipment, and their mom, who was selling T-shirts." Greenberg was sold. So much so that he offered Hanson a recording contract right then and there.

With no time to celebrate, Hanson was flown to Los Angeles, where the family again temporarily relocated, to spend the next five months recording what would be their debut CD for Mercury Records. Mercury hooked Hanson up with some of the best songwriters and producers in the business to ensure that its first record would have all the right ingredients for success.

THE MAKING OF *MIDDLE OF NOWHERE*

Writer-producer Steve Lironi (who'd worked with the British bands Space and Black Grape) and John King and Michael Simpson, better known as the Dust Brothers (who produced Beck's Grammy Award–winning *Odelay*), were hired by Greenberg to produce the record. Mark Hudson, formerly of a brotherly singing group himself, '70s stars the Hudson Brothers, was brought in to cowrite some of the new songs with Hanson. Hudson had previously written "Living on the Edge" for Aerosmith. Greenberg also brought in songwriters Ellen Shipley (Belinda Carlisle's "Heaven Is a Place on Earth"), Desmond Child (several Bon Jovi and Aerosmith songs), and the duo Barry Mann and Cynthia Weil (the Righteous Brothers' "You've Lost That Lovin' Feeling") to lend a hand.

Three songs from *MMMBop* were to be included on the debut, including the title track, "With You in Your Dreams" (an emotional song about the Hanson boys' late grandmother), and "Thinking of You." The bonus track, "Man from Milwaukee," available as an extra thirteenth song on the CD version only, was also penned by Isaac, Taylor, and Zachary alone. The name of the debut, *Middle of Nowhere*, was taken from a lyric in "Man from Milwaukee."

Hudson cowrote three songs on the album with Hanson, including "Where's the Love," "A Minute Without You," and "Lucy." Lironi had a hand in "Speechless" and "Look at You," while Mann and Weil collaborated with Hanson on the romantic ballad "I Will Come to You." Ike, Tay, and Zac worked with Child on "Weird," an idea they had because it's a word the brothers like to use a lot. Shipley helped them write "Yearbook," a song about a missing classmate. When asked what his favorite song on *Middle of Nowhere* was, Zac said, "I cannot betray a song. We love all the songs. They're all too valuable."

Throughout the recording process, all the helping hands proved invaluable to Hanson, ensuring the boys maintained a positive attitude while creating a quality record. In many ways, Hudson acted as a mentor to Hanson, offering advice and encouragement along the way. At the same time, the Dust Brothers helped keep it fun. Some of the sessions were done at the Dust Brothers' house, where they maintain an impressive recording studio with top-notch equipment. When things got tense or the boys needed a break, the Dust Brothers would invite Ike, Tay, and Zac for a swim in their pool. "We jumped in with our clothes on," Zac remembers.

"MMMBOP" TILL YOU DROP

Hanson originally came up with "MMMBop" nearly four years ago. It was supposed to be just a chorus for another song, but after a while, Zac and his bros found a way to make it a song all on its own. While the chorus to the song makes it sound inane, Zac explains that "MMMBop" has deeper meaning than most people realize. "It's about holding on to the ones who really care, which might be your brothers and sisters if you have them."

The version of "MMMBop" that made it onto *Middle of Nowhere,* however, was a little different from the original. With some assistance from the producing team, Hanson sped up the pace of the song to turn it into the infectious and rhythmic, jump-up-and-down song that we all know today. Many music writers have gone so far as to say "MMMBop" is the most irresistible pop song since the Jackson Five's "ABC." It was the ideal choice for a first single.

AT LONG LAST—SUCCESS!

Mercury Records was so confident in the single that they released it for radio play on March 24, 1997, nearly two months before the May release of *Middle of Nowhere*. Within days, "MMMBop" became one of the most listener-requested songs on the radio, and in late April, when the single was made available in record stores, it debuted at number sixteen on the *Billboard* charts, earning it Hot Shot Debut honors. "MMMBop" climbed to number six the following week, then to two, and by May 24, it was number one. By the Fourth of July, it had been unofficially anointed 1997's summer anthem.

The Hanson boys were blown away. When *Teen Beat* asked Zac if he'd expected their first single to be so successful, he said, "You can't expect this. You hope for it, but . . ."

33

When a reporter asked Hanson how they planned to celebrate the success of "MMM-Bop," Isaac suggested a party with all their friends, and Taylor laughed and said, "Jump up and down!" Zac interrupted with, "Get girlfriends!" and then, more seriously, he suggested, "Go to Laser Quest and play . . . like fifty times!"

SEEING "MMMBOP" IS BELIEVING

In today's era of music, a music video is nearly as important to the success of a song as the amount of radio play it gets. After all, the young CD-buying market spends as much time watching MTV as listening to the radio. Understanding the importance of making a great video, Mercury put the project in the hands of young, hip, and up-and-coming director Tamra Davis. Davis had previously made videos for alternative groups Sonic Youth and Luscious Jackson.

Davis chose Los Angeles as the video location, and throughout the filming, she maintained a loose atmosphere and always asked the boys for their input. "We were acting weird, and she would say, 'Just do that in slow motion' or something," Zac recalls. Davis had a vision of making a video that would capture the playfulness and carefree spirit of Hanson.

Meanwhile, Zac and his brothers were looking to make it fun, so the match-up was perfect.

The Hanson brothers really did have as good a time as it appears in the video for "MMMBop." In fact, they did all their own stunts. "The skating wipeout was real. Definitely all real," Zac admitted.

Davis confessed, "Zac definitely falls down a lot!"

Davis originally had wanted the brothers to ride bikes, but Ike, Tay, and Zac suggested the whole idea of jumping from cab to bus to the Humvee car they drive around in. (The car was actually used in the movie *Speed 2,* and no, Taylor is not really driving it!) The beach, the cave, and all the running around and Rollerblading made the video fun to watch as well. Mercury Records and Hanson alike were so pleased with how the video came out that they would later rehire Davis to film their second video, "Where's the Love," in England.

HANSONMANIA!

The next step, and it was a huge one, was to introduce Hanson to America. "MMMBop" put the name "Hanson" on the tips of our collective tongues, but it was the May 6, 1997, release of *Middle of Nowhere* that sounded the starting gun on the band's race to be famous. Fueled by the popularity of "MMMBop," *Middle of Nowhere* entered the *Billboard* charts at number six. Immediately after the debut disc hit record-store shelves, Mercury Records brought its new darlings to New York for a tornado of press interviews, photo shoots, mini-performances, and talk-show appearances.

The most sleepless week in the boys' lives began with what was supposed to be a "little

36

promo performance" in the Paramus Park mall. Z-100, New York's most popular Top 40 radio station, sponsored the event that was mapped out to have Hanson play two songs on a makeshift stage inside the mall and then field a few questions from deejay Cubby Bryant. Because the appearance hadn't been advertised or heavily publicized, mall security had prepared for only a few hundred people to show up. When that many were already lined up five hours before Hanson was due to arrive, security called for backup.

By the time eight o'clock A.M. rolled around and the Hansons made their way toward their instruments, an estimated six thousand fans had packed not only the area around the ministage but every escalator and staircase in sight! "It was pretty crazy!" Zac recalls. "We were nervous because previously, the biggest crowd we'd played in front of was a couple of hundred, maybe, but not six thousand!" Hanson's two-song set was over in a flash, that is, if anyone was lucky enough to hear a note over the thunder and lightning of fan excitement. With security unable to control the crowd, the Hanson brothers had to exit without doing the interview. Ike, Tay, and Zac had gotten their first dose of Hansonmania. "Having fans wait hours and hours to see you, that's pretty awesome," Zac says.

FULL-COURT PRESS

Appropriately, Hanson's weeklong New York media roller coaster began with the *Rosie O'Donnell* show. Aside from having one of the top-rated talk shows on television, O'Donnell has won the trust of young celebrities (she and Jonathan Taylor Thomas are mutual fans) and their fans with her role in the movie *Harriet the Spy* and her involvement with Nickelodeon's "The Big Help" and other children's charities. *Rosie* proved to be the perfect way for the Hansons to show their media savvy. O'Donnell persuaded the studio audience to clap along as the boys played "MMMBop," and she later complimented them on their adorable looks, manners, and talent. Who could blame her?

After *Rosie*, Hanson spent the next three days being blitzed by the print media. One after another, Hanson answered questions from journalists at *Rolling Stone, Spin, Entertainment Weekly, Teen Beat, 16, Tiger Beat, Interview, People, US,* and even *Time* and *Newsweek.* During one busy day in Central Park, Ike, Tay, and Zac were doing a photo shoot for *Seventeen* at the same time as they were being interviewed by MTV! When the MTV reporter asked Zac if he was the ham of the group, he cracked, "No, I'm the chicken!" Even in Central Park, away from the traffic and busy sidewalks, Hanson's presence did not go unnoticed. "In New York, while we were doing a photo shoot, there was a crowd following us," Zac remembers. "That was pretty cool."

Next, the boys did on-camera interviews for MTV, VH-1, *Access Hollywood,* and *Entertainment Tonight.* Following that were TV appearances on *The Jenny Jones Show, CBS This Morning,* the *Today* show, *Live with Regis and Kathie Lee,* and *The Late Show with David Letterman.* The last one was a biggie for the boys as they're all big fans, especially Zac. "It's Letterman! It's like, whoa, why would Letterman want us?" he wondered. "But if he wants us, I'll go."

As if there wasn't enough excitement for Ike, Tay, and Zac that week, "MMMBop" reached number one on the *Billboard* charts. That day, May 26, was declared Hanson Day in Oklahoma. When Kathie Lee Gifford asked the boys what it was like to receive the honor from Governor Frank Keating, Zac and Taylor answered, "Actually, we didn't, because we were here to do *Letterman!"*

When Isaac, Taylor, and Zachary finally left the Big Apple, it was off to Los Angeles for more of the same. Hanson began week two with another wave of hysteria, this time at the Sam Goody record store at Universal City Walk. This time, the blond trio was better prepared, and so was the security. Although they attracted two thousand fans to the store and the crowd noise was enough to make the windows shake, Hanson was able to squeeze in a short interview before the four-song set. Things went smoothly compared to Paramus, but still not smoothly enough for the Hanson brothers to stick around and sign autographs. It was a quick exit, something the boys were growing accustomed to.

FAME AND FIFTH GRADE

When *16* magazine asked Zac, "What advice do you have for kids who want to do what you do?" he answered, "It's a lot of work! Once you get a record deal, it doesn't stop there." While many of his peers may be jealous of Zac's success and fame, the twelve-year-old had to endure quite a bit during his band's meteoric rise.

Indeed, Zac has had to make plenty of sacrifices to do what he does. During an interview with MTV, when *Middle of Nowhere* had just come out and Hansonmania was just beginning, Zac complained, "We haven't been home in like a month!" Traveling the world to perform, film videos, do interviews, and record songs takes its toll on any musician, but

41

how about on a sixth-grader? As if expending all that energy on flights, jet lag, and hectic scheduling isn't enough, Zac also misses his home, family, and friends back in Tulsa. "Some friends gave us a big [snow] globe of Tulsa that we take with us on the road. It reminds us of home."

After their whirlwind publicity and promotion tour last spring and right before they'd embark on more of the same overseas, Hanson was about to take a short break. When the brothers were asked what they were looking forward to doing, Ike and Tay mentioned seeing family and friends, while Zac answered, "Sleep!"

As much as Zac appreciates his fans and enjoys performing and traveling, he does look forward to taking some time off for himself. Hanson planned on squeezing in a week off around Christmas to go back to Tulsa and spend some time at home with the family and, of course, go to Laser Quest! But, even before that, the guys needed a little peace and quiet. "We're going to go to this lake and rent a house—you know, one of those little apartment things," Zac describes. "And then we're gonna just unplug the phone!"

Despite Zac's ultra-high energy level, he's still a kid, and kids get tired, too. Louis Drapp, who owned the studio where Hanson recorded its second independent release, *MMMBop,* told a Tulsa reporter, "After recording for a couple of hours, the little drummer would get real tired. He played great, and then, like, all of a sudden, he'd start playing quieter. And I'm like, where'd the snare go? He'd still be hitting it, but at different levels because he was getting tired. Drumming takes a lot of energy anyway, and then at his age, well, that's hard on a kid!" At that point, the Hanson bros would take a break and order some pizza.

"They'd bring some toys with them and play," Drapp recalls. "Game Boy–type things and some Transformers—at least the little one, not the big ones. They would bring pencils and paper." Drapp remembers Zac as fun-loving and spontaneous. "He's very outgoing—on the spur of the moment. He's the one who'll just be quiet and then just cuts up, you know. He just has fun."

BRING IN THE NOISE

Zac has often referred to the growing legion of screaming young female Hanson fans as "the Scream Squad." "It's really cool to think people are screaming at you," but, Zac says, "sometimes we can't hear ourselves think." It's a little-known fact that the Hanson brothers wear earplugs onstage during every performance. Other bands do so as well to drown out the blare of the nearby speakers. The Hanson brothers, on the other hand, do so to dim the piercing screams from their excited fans!

During a performance in front of a small crowd after appearing on the *Today* show in New York, Zac told photographer Ernie Paniccioli, "What good is it if we are a hit and we lose our hearing? Those girls should calm down a bit!"

Paniccioli answered him, "If each girl buys a CD, you'll be well off."

"Not if we're deaf!" Zac snapped back.

Zac, of course, doesn't really want the crowds to quiet down. After all, he's the one who's always trying to rile them up. What he means is that it can be frustrating trying to maintain a tempo and stay in tune with his brothers when the crowd noise competes with the music. Many bands have had trouble with this early on in their careers. In time, Zac and his brothers will get the hang of it.

GROUNDED IN SUCCESS

"When we were signed [by Mercury Records], it was just kinda like, you saw it in the paper and you just kinda go, 'OK,'" Zac recalls. "It's kinda like, when I turn twelve, I'm just gonna go, 'I'm twelve.'" Maybe it hadn't all sunk in for Zac at that point. But a year and six million copies later, Zac has had to maintain his cool to prevent it all from going to his head.

One thing that has helped young Zac deal with all the attention is keeping things in perspective. After a newspaper article compared Hanson to the Beatles, Zac reacted, "The Beatles? I mean, they were the *Beatles!*" When another feature referred to the brothers as the "next big thing," Zac said, "Being the next big thing, that's just a good line, I guess you would say. We don't necessarily think we're the big shots."

In fact, through all the hype and hoopla, Zac and his brothers have remained humble. When asked what it's like being stars, Taylor answers, "People think of us as stars, and we don't think we're stars at all. Not even for a second."

Zac adds his silly take on the subject. "We think, Stars? Where?" Not that Zac doesn't get excited about Hanson's level of success. "It's really cool seeing ourselves on MTV. It's awesome to look and go, 'That's me!' It's a great feeling."

During an America Online interview, Zac was asked by a fan, "What's the best part about being in a popular group?" Zac responded, "I don't know. You're the same person. The best part is getting the experience and getting to go to the different places. We've already gotten the chance to go to Europe and Japan. We've gotten a great opportunity." At the end of the AOL interview, Zac showed that, more than anything, Hanson's fans make it all worth it. Zac signed off at the end of the on-line chat by saying, "We love you people, and thanks for talking to us. It's great to know someone's out there."

PLAYIN' IN A TRAVELIN' BAND

It's not easy being on the road. Your friends are thousands of miles away in Tulsa, Oklahoma. You're exhausted from jumping from trains to planes to taxis, and you sleep in a different bed almost every night, never your own. However, Isaac, Taylor, and Zachary made the most of their excursions. They made new friends in every city they visited and took in many of the world's most famous sights. "Touring Europe is awesome!" Zac proclaims. "We can see all these places in real life instead of just looking at a book." Although the boys are home-schooled, there is one book that's required. Dad Walker always encouraged his boys to record their experiences, so Zac and his brothers bring a

47

journal with them wherever they go to jot down the sights they see and the things they learn.

Just because the Hanson brothers are home-schooled doesn't mean they can't have some great learning experiences outside their home—or country, for that matter. Isaac, Taylor and Zachary use their time in foreign countries wisely, often as a good excuse for a history lesson. Being on the road is hard enough for any musician, but for three young rockers like Hanson, it's double duty! Not only do they have to greet fans and meet with the foreign press, but they also have to keep up with their studies. They don't have to worry about missing any tests, though. It's a good thing the Hansons are home-schooled, since their successes seem to keep them on the road.

FAR OUT IN THE FAR EAST

Of all the places the Hanson brothers have visited, the Far East has to be the most exotic so far. Even the gifts they received from fans had an Asian twist. Ike, Tay, and Zac appreciated getting pairs of traditional wooden clogs from their Japanese fans, even if they were "kinda hard to walk on." Hanson's tour of the Far East included stops in Korea, Taiwan, and Hong Kong.

Hansonmania struck in Tokyo, when, during a radio station interview, so many more fans showed up than were expected that they had to be escorted by Japanese officials past the band one group at a time. But that was just an appetizer compared to the way Australian fans were about to devour Hanson!

It didn't take long to realize that Hansonmania had stricken the Land Down Under as well. Ike, Tay, and Zac were swamped by fans at the airport before they even got to their hotel. The brothers first visited Sydney, where they did some press interviews and then a few promotional appearances, one of which was a live performance on a boat ride full of fans!

Thousands came to enjoy Hanson's performance outside the Westfield Mall in Melbourne, Australia's second-largest city. The young Australians pushed and shoved to fit as many people as possible in the parking-lot area near the stage. When the show and the subsequent standing ovation were over, Ike, Tay, and Zac needed a police escort to get through the mall! Hanson's week in the land of kangaroos and koalas concluded with a few days' rest. "You gotta pace yourself," Zac says. After a few *zzz*'s and some more touring, it was on to Europe. When the whole world wants you, there's little time for rest.

CIAO, HANSON!

Hanson made short but sweet trips to Italy, Germany, and France. The brothers did meet-and-greets, mini-performances and, naturally, more press. They did the usual interviews, but the European press had some different questions in mind. After an interview with *Bravo* magazine, Germany's answer to *16* and *Teen Beat,* Radio/Libre in Paris was next. When a French reporter offered comparisons to the Jackson Five, she suggested Zachary was the Michael of the group. "Aaaaah!" he screamed.

"So, you intend to do plastic surgery?" she asked him.

"No! I like my face the way it is," he responded.

Southern Europe was mostly work, but the boys found time for some sightseeing as well. Zac seemed especially to enjoy the European sights. His highlights? "Italy has great food. In France, seeing the Eiffel Tower. In Germany, the Dom Cathedral."

CROSSING THE ENGLISH CHANNEL

"We love the U.K.!" Zac proclaimed to *Entertainment Weekly* during an exclusive overseas photo shoot and interview. Little did Zac know that quote would end up inside an issue of the big-time mag that would feature him and his bros on the cover! The publicity wouldn't end there, however.

In London, Hanson was interviewed by British magazines *The Face* and *Smash Hits* and then by BBC-Radio 1. Zac was being his usual silly self throughout the question-and-answer period and got particularly unruly when the interviewer neglected him and only addressed his brothers. This led to a brief discussion over the origins of his nickname, "Animal." Later, when the interviewer asked what the boys would choose to be if they weren't musicians, Zac answered, "I would be Zac the . . . I don't know."

"Zac the Muppet?" the interviewer asked.

"I most likely would be very calm, actually," Zac replied with a straight face.

During a Q&A session with *Smash Hits* magazine, Zac responded to a question about missing out on school, friends, and an ordinary childhood. "We're experiencing new people and new cultures. Things like the London Dungeons and the Tower of London history ride. How many U.S. history teachers would die to be able to send their class to London?" Good point, Zac.

Of course, no trip to England could be complete without a shopping spree, right?

"The whole Hanson family went shopping," Zac proudly admits. "We all went to the big Doc Marten shoe store in London, and we all bought some boots. So every time you come into our hotel room, all you can see is different-colored boots everywhere!"

How does Zac sum up his adventures abroad? "It was awesome!" Does Zac have a favorite city abroad? "I've enjoyed all the places we've been," he concludes. And it goes without saying that he and his brothers were adored everywhere they went.

ZAC

(Ernie Paniccioli/Retna)

HANSON

(Ernie Paniccioli/Retna)

ZAC ATTACK!

(David Atlas/Retna)

(Ernest Paniccioli/Shooting Star)

(Ernie Paniccioli/Retna)

(P. Adress/A.P.R.F./Shooting Star)

(Celebrity Photo Agency)

ONE CRAZY SUMMER

Hanson returned to the United States with a full round of appearances and performances to squeeze into a month. The first stop was Los Angeles, where the brothers had two places to be. The first was as the musical guest on *The Tonight Show with Jay Leno*. This normally would have been a landmark opportunity for Isaac, Taylor, and Zachary, but with so many talk shows under their belts at this point, they didn't bat an eye, despite performing for millions of TV viewers on the highest-rated late-night show.

Their next gig, however, was a very big deal. Hanson made its debut as presenters at the *MTV Movie Awards*. You would think being in a theater full of movie stars and big-time

53

celebs would make Ike, Tay, and Zac nervous, but funnyman David Spade was there to break the ice. The former *Saturday Night Live* "buh-bye" guy and Chris Farley sidekick came on-stage with the brothers and pretended to be the fourth member of the group, announcing, "Hi, we're Hanson." Isaac and Taylor broke out in huge grins, and Zac burst out laughing. The rest was a snap.

BACK TO THE BIG APPLE

The brothers flew to New York once again and created a stir downtown when their appearance on *FOX After Breakfast* turned into an outdoor street concert that attracted hundreds of young fans. After the talk segment, which was sandwiched between interviews with *Suddenly Susan*'s Kathy Griffin and veteran actor Peter Fonda, was completed, Hanson and crew set up a mini-stage on the street corner outside the building where the show is filmed in New York City's Flatiron District. It was already ninety-five degrees out that July day, but when Hanson broke into an unexpected live show, the sidewalks really sizzled! After "MMMBop," "Where's the Love," and a few minutes of screaming, clapping, and stamping were over, Ike, Tay, and Zac showed their New York fans the meaning of consideration. As hordes of girls reached out their hands to touch them and hordes of others held out posters to be signed, the boys took a few moments to meet the fans and sign autographs. After things got out of hand, however, they were rushed into their limos and headed off for the airport.

MIDDLE OF AMERICA

There were several stops throughout the Midwest on this installment of the promotional tour. Fans in Detroit, Oklahoma City, Charlotte, and Minneapolis all got a taste of the MMMBoppin' sensations. Hanson mayhem struck again when the brothers rocked for charity at Bloomington, Minnesota's famous Mall of America. On a typical day, hundreds of teens flock to America's biggest shopping mall to check out all the cool stores and amusement rides. Hundreds became thousands when a certain band came to perform a live show in the parking lot!

The gig was held as part of Jam Against Hunger, a series of concerts benefiting hunger and flood relief. Hanson's parking-lot concert was free, but everyone who attended was asked to bring a nonperishable food item to help the needy. Hanson, the biggest mall in the country, and a great charity benefit all wrapped up in one sounds too good to be true, but if anyone could pull it off, it's the Brothers H!

AROUND THE WORLD . . . AND BACK AGAIN

Before completing their first summer of love in America, the Hansons hopped a jet to England again, this time to film their next video. Their second single, "Where's the Love," the hardest-rockin' track from *Middle of Nowhere* and a song that some music writers feel is even more infectious than "MMM-Bop," would need a great video to capture its energy. Tamra Davis, who directed the video for "MMMBop," again would lead the way. Two weeks earlier, the boys had met with Davis to discuss some of their ideas for the video. When Isaac, Taylor, and Zachary arrived on the set, they were excited, Davis says. "They wanted to shoot in a warehouse, and when they got there, they saw it was exactly what they wanted." Davis was impressed with how the boys had been handling their success since they had worked together on the last video. "They laughed about it, saying, 'We'd be really crazy if we changed in two weeks!'"

TENNIS, ANYONE?

Meanwhile, back in the homeland, extensive radio play had made "MMMBop" the summer anthem. How appropriate! The U.S. Tennis Association gave Hanson a perfect way to celebrate its achievements by inviting the group to perform for the grand opening of Arthur Ashe Stadium, where the U.S. Open would later be played. The first annual Arthur Ashe Kids' Day attracted more than twenty thousand fans to the National Tennis Center in Flushing, New York. Some came to get a close-up look at the best tennis players in the world, others came for the many interactive clinics and prize giveaways, but the majority of the fans were on hand to watch their favorite band perform.

Arthur Ashe Kids' Day honored the late tennis star for his achievements on and off the court while benefiting the Arthur Ashe Foundation and other charitable organizations. The event was spearheaded by an in-stadium program hosted by Bill Cosby that featured mini-matches between some of tennis's best pros and an appearance by *Nickelodeon* stars Kenan Thompson and Kel Mitchell. But the highlight of the day by far was Hanson's performance. The brothers first came out to play "MMMBop" and "Where's the Love," songs that were barely audible above the piercing screams from the crowd. After the day's events were supposed to be over, Hanson came back out for a bonus set that sent the fans into a frenzy! When asked what it was like to have thousands of girls screaming for him, Zac replied, "It's awesome!"

After their first set, Ike, Tay, and Zac were supposed to play a scheduled tennis match with the number one women's player Martina Hingis, but stormy skies held things up a bit. The Hansons, not the greatest tennis players, considered themselves fortunate. "We were just hoping we could hit the ball," Zac remarked.

Hundreds of girls dashed around the stadium walkways in search of Hanson's dressing room. They never did find it, but at one point they all stopped dead in their tracks and almost toppled like dominoes. After a brief pause, the group let out one long, collective shriek when they realized that Isaac, Taylor, and Zachary were standing right in front of them. At first, the fans were disappointed that the guys only signed a few autographs, but had they known at the time that Hanson needed to get ready for their secret bonus set, they wouldn't have minded at all.

MAKING THE "SCREAM SQUAD" FAMOUS

Hanson closed out its commotion-filled summer with a unique performance that would give some of its fans a shot at fame. To come up with live footage for a long-format video, *Tulsa, Tokyo and the Middle of Nowhere,* Hanson held a special concert at New York City's famed Beacon Theater. No tickets were sold, but a few hundred fortunate fans from the area who won radio contests got invited to this exciting event.

While Ike, Tay, and Zac were getting ready backstage, the cameras focused on the energized crowd as they bellowed, "We want Hanson!" When Taylor came onto center stage and yelled, "Are you ready to rock?" the theater filled with screams. Then Zachary and Isaac came running onstage shooting Silly String into the crowd. Hanson played a six-song set that ended with an unplugged version of "MMMBop."

Afterward, Mercury Records president Danny Goldberg came onstage to present Hanson with a fifth platinum record, meaning *Middle of Nowhere* had sold more than five million copies (by now it's more than six million). Minutes later, Ike, Tay, and Zac came back onstage in new outfits to film a video for "I Will Come to You." The audience was thrilled to see more of Hanson live, and also to realize that they were a part of a new video!

ZACHARY'S ZANY ANTICS

"I think it's probably because I'm so shy that I just act wacky to make up for it." Nice try, Zac. There's no denying it, not even by Zac himself, that he's the most outgoing, risk-taking, and flat-out wackiest member of Hanson.

"It's really amazing," Taylor explains, "because Zac acts crazy and wild, but he'll be, like, really quiet, too."

Throughout Hanson's touring, interviewing, traveling, and even recording, Zac's antics have been well documented. Whether he's doing something crazy to get the crowd excited at a show or just trying to push his older brothers' buttons, there's no slowing him down. As Taylor tells it, "Zac's the drummer, so he'll go, 'I'm the drummer, and I'll do whatever I want,' so he'll speed us up, slow us down, whatever he wants to do."

During *Meet Hanson*, the ABC *American Bandstand* special that aired Thanksgiving weekend, host Dick Clark asked the boys, "If you have a problem between you, how do you solve it?"

"We kill each other!" Zac yelled, and then jumped up and down, pretending to punch Isaac.

The fun doesn't end at his brothers' expense, however. Not even close. Zac has just as much fun with the crowd. At the Paramus, New Jersey, show, Zac yelled to the crowd, "Could you all be quiet? You're hurting my ears! Keep it down, girls. I'm going to lose my hearing! Keep it down!"

When fans approach Zac, the fun continues. "Somebody's bigger sister once said, 'Will you go out with my little sister?' I was like, 'I don't go out with people yet.'"

Zac also gets a kick out of torturing other celebrities. When the Hansons made an appearance on *FOX After Breakfast,* they were the second guests to come on, following *Suddenly Susan*'s Kathy Griffin. Griffin, a spunky live wire herself, joked with the Hansons about taking one of them on as her next boyfriend. Zac snapped back with a comment referring to her age, and then Griffin retorted with another zinger. The rip session went back and forth until Zac found a surefire way to win. He flung doughnuts at Griffin while she was on camera!

The most fun Zac has, by far, however, is during interviews. More than anything, Zac likes to make jokes at the expense of journalists. A popular question that reporters often ask celebrities is, "If you weren't a star, what would you be doing?" Zac likes to yuk it up with this question. His responses to it have varied from "I want to be a worker in a Burger King" to "I would be very calm, actually" to screaming, "I just wanna be in a band called Hanson!"

When a writer for *Tiger Beat* magazine asked Zac what his favorite color was, he snapped, "Blue, why are you asking me that?" Zac also likes to kid reporters that his parents forced him and his brothers into a musical career, he and his brothers all despise each other, and they're only in it for the money. When you meet Zac, it doesn't take long to realize that he's as quick with sarcasm as he is with his drumsticks. Zac's mischief may be considered out of control by some, but without it, Hanson would be missing something.

ONE-LINERS

Managing the responsibilities of his career has matured Zac a great deal. Spending so much time around adults and so much time in foreign lands has made him wise beyond his years. However, he never lets us lose sight of how old he really is, occasionally spewing out some of the most ridiculous comments. Luckily for Zac, twelve-year-olds can get away with saying certain things that real adults can't. As sharp as he is, Zac knows that full well, and don't think he doesn't take advantage of it. Here's Zac in some of his vintage moments:

"I find it weird when fans scream at us because they want to meet us. When we actually go over and talk to them, they say nothing. They just look at us and go, 'Er, um.' That's weird."

"We've gotten a good response from old guys, too—college guys."

"Look at that cute girl—no, wait, it's me!"

"I like to bang on things."

"Think of us as old people with high voices."

"I'm five foot one, but that's not exact."

"I'm goofy stupid."

"I have a lot of favorite foods, but now I'd just like a big pile of Jell-O."

"The Dust Brothers have a very clean house."

"We don't have as many problems as grown-ups!"

"They're trying to make us look taller, but it's just not working."

"Someone got our name wrong and called us Handsome!"

"I'm not gonna get married in the next five or six years."

OUT WITH A BANG

If Hanson's 1997 began with hype and home-grown fame, it ended with fireworks and fanfare. The blond brothers celebrated the conclusion of their first big year as pop stars with a slew of TV appearances and two new projects.

In late September, Hanson kicked off ABC's new season of TGIF (the Friday-night lineup that features popular kids' sitcoms) with a special presentation of *Sabrina, the Teenage Witch, Boy Meets World, You Wish,* and *Teen Angel.* Between shows, the brothers put their own unique twist on introducing each episode. Fans of the TGIF shows were treated to Hanson's hunky faces and Zac's token wisecracks as they welcomed ABC's new season.

65

Ike, Tay, and Zac followed that up with their most special performance to date. The three were given the honor of singing the national anthem for the World Series in Miami. Hanson crooned in front of about sixty thousand fans, not to mention about twenty million TV viewers! Major League Baseball's ratings got a boost that night as thousands of teenage girls tuned in right along with all the sports fans. Not everyone was interested in just the Cleveland Indians versus the Florida Marlins. In fact, many Hanson fans probably changed the channel (and pressed stop on the VCR) right before the first pitch was even thrown!

Hanson's next stop was Holland, for the MTV Europe Music Awards. The brothers' role in the ceremony was threefold: they were presenters and performers as well as award recipients. In the end, the long plane ride was well worth it as they took home awards for Best Breakthrough Act and Best Song for "MMMBop," which they got to play for the delighted crowd. Other award recipients included the Backstreet Boys and the Spice Girls, whom Hanson got to meet afterward. "They're all short," Zac remarked when he noticed that Emma "Baby Spice" Bunton, Taylor's favorite Spice Girl, was about his height.

FROM ROCK STARS TO TV STARS

After returning to the United States, Hanson made four national TV appearances within a span of just three weeks. First was a November 28 ABC special all about them called *Meet Hanson*. The half-hour special was hosted by the legendary Dick Clark as part of his long-running music series, *American Bandstand*. Clark began the show with a Hanson Q&A session, followed by a rockin' performance of "MMMBop." The boys added acoustic versions of "Madeline," "Man from Milwaukee," and "I Will Come to You," as well as a medley of Christmas songs. Between songs, Isaac, Taylor, and Zachary spoke to their fans about the kind of year they'd had and the meaning behind a few of their songs.

An expression of pride was evident on little Zac's mug as his brothers explained the origin of "Man from Milwaukee." That proud look soon turned to one of embarrassment, however, when Isaac shared a story about Zac jumping into the crowd at one show, only to emerge with a wedgie! As the show ended, Ike, Tay, and Zac thanked their fans for a great year. "Thanks to you guys, we've gotten to travel the world and see some amazing things," Zac concluded.

Two weeks after the ABC special Hanson

returned to New York to be the musical guest on *Saturday Night Live*. On December 19, their last day of "work" before the brothers would head back to Tulsa for the holidays and some much-needed rest, Hanson made two special appearances. Hanson fans woke up to Isaac, Taylor, and Zachary on ABC's *Good Morning, America* and then were serenaded to sleep by the group's special performance that night for *Christmas in Washington*.

A VERY HANSON CHRISTMAS

During this time, Hanson's third single and most beautiful ballad, "I Will Come to You," began getting radio play. The video, which features fans from the Beacon Theater performance, soon followed. Ike, Tay, and Zac also found time for an America Online interview and the introduction of a line of Hanson merchandise, including T-shirts, posters, stickers, and a calendar. But by far the most exciting Hanson news to close out 1997 was what the trio calls "our Christmas gifts to the fans."

The first gift was the Hanson video, *Tulsa, Tokyo, and the Middle of Nowhere*. Fans were treated to a firsthand look at the brothers together on the road, in the studio, and at home. The keepsake tape features highlights from the group's exciting year, including concert footage, fan hysteria, TV appearances, photo shoots, traveling, and, best of all, some behind-the-scenes fun with Ike, Tay, and Zac. Four of the live tracks were recorded at New York City's Beacon Theater, so fans who were lucky enough to attend got to see themselves on film! A special bonus segment included a cappella and acoustic versions of a few songs, with guest appearances by celebrities like Cindy Crawford and Weird Al Yankovic. More than a few Hanson fans probably found a copy of *Tulsa, Tokyo, and the Middle of Nowhere* in their Christmas stockings.

Speaking of Christmas, Hanson's other gift to fans was the release of *Snowed In,* the trio's first holiday album. They recorded *Snowed In* in October in a countryside studio in Berkshire, England. British teen mag *Smash Hits* was on hand for an informal interview. "We're really in the Christmas mood at the moment," Zac told the reporter. "Last night, to celebrate finishing the album, we had a Christmas dinner!"

Isaac, Taylor, and Zachary made their second major recording a Yuletide celebration, with their take on some merry classics as well as three brand-new holiday-themed songs of their own. The inside cover of the CD features festive shots of Ike, Tay, and Zac frolicking in the snow and wrapped in holiday lights, as well as a personal message to their fans. It closes with "Thanks for sharing your holiday season with us." (You're very welcome!)

On the record, Hanson adds its own flavor to Yuletide staples such as "Merry Christmas Baby," "What Christmas Means to Me," "Little Saint Nick," "Christmas (Baby Please Come Home)," "Rockin' Around the Christmas Tree," "Run Rudolph Run," and even "White Christmas." Zac sings lead on "What Christmas Means to Me" and "Rockin' Around the Christmas Tree." The best cover song, however, is the "Silent Night Medley," which includes "O Holy Night," "Silent Night," and "O Come All Ye Faithful" all rolled into one. The brothers take turns at the mike for the first and last part, but they produce one of their most beautiful harmonies yet in their rendition of "Silent Night." *Snowed In* also includes Hanson's contribution to Christmas posterity with "At Christmas," "Christmas Time," and "Everybody Knows the Claus." Hanson gave its fans a taste of *Snowed In* at the end of the *Meet Hanson* TV special.

HANSON LIVE!

Hanson found the time and energy to perform twenty live shows from mid-October through mid-December for big-city radio station promotions. Two of the more memorable performances included the Halloween show for Chicago's B-96 FM and the mid-November show in Miami for the annual Wing Ding fund-raiser concert. At both shows, Hanson shared the stage with other great acts, including the Backstreet Boys, Robyn, En Vogue, and Ziggy Marley and the Melody Makers.

South Florida's biggest Top 40 radio station, Y-100 (serving Miami, Palm Beach, and Fort Lauderdale), held its eleventh annual Wing Ding concert series at Hollywood's Young Circle Park on the weekend of November 15. The event benefited Here's Help, a nonprofit agency that helps fight drug abuse. Featuring the participation of area restaurants in a chicken wing recipe competition, Y-100's Wing Ding attracts tons of celebrities, as well as thousands of fans. At this past year's festival, fans were treated to appearances by professional athletes, actors, and comedians and performances by ten different bands. Hanson and fellow rockers drew such a turnout that for the first time ever, the event had to be spread out over two days.

TRICK OR TREAT?

While Hanson was recording *Snowed In,* the brothers joked with *Smash Hits* magazine about their Halloween plans. "We're still going to go trick-or-treating this year!" Zac proclaimed. "It's not like someone's gonna see us," he pointed out. "We'll be all dressed up with masks on. Then you go around getting tons of candy!" Zac then explained the importance of Halloween in America by joking, "It used to be like, 'Gimme a treat, or I'll set your house on fire!'" As it turned out, Zac's elaborate plans would have to be put on the back burner. (No pun intended.)

When Hanson teamed up with the Backstreet Boys for a Halloween promotional concert for Chicago's B-96 FM radio station, they sold out the Rosemont Horizon arena. Fans lucky enough to get tickets to this once-in-a-lifetime event were treated to an unbelievable show that also featured performances by Robyn, Le Clique, and En Vogue. The arena featured big-screen monitors, so everyone could get a close-up look at Hanson, no doubt, as well as festive decorations such as glowing plastic skeletons. Zachary added to the Halloween theme by performing in costume, sporting a bright yellow motorcycle outfit with his hair in braids. As if the show weren't magical enough, Hanson stuck around afterward to sign autographs and pose for pictures with fans!

CLOSING OUT '97

To get an idea of how busy they were at this time, check out Hanson's schedule from November 19 through December 10. On the nineteenth, Hanson performed a few songs in the morning for Detroit's W-KQI and W-DRQ radio stations and then headed to Cleveland for a nighttime appearance on W-QAL and W-ZJM. They topped themselves by fitting in three gigs in twenty-four hours the following day. Washington, D.C.'s W-WZZ featured them in the morning, then Baltimore's W-XYV had afternoon honors, and Hanson still made it to Philadelphia for an evening performance for W-IOQ. Before they could catch their breath, Ike, Tay, and Zac had another triple-header the next day! First up was Pittsburgh's W-BZZ, then Columbus, Ohio's W-NCI, and, last, a quick flight down to Atlanta capped off the day with an appearance on W-STR's *Celebrity Rock Cafe Show*. Whew!

After a weeklong break to catch up on sleep, Hanson made a dazzling return to the Big Apple for what would be its biggest show yet—Z-100's Jingle Ball at Madison Square Garden. The event, which featured other groups as well, easily sold out New York City's famous twenty-thousand-seat arena. If this were a year ago, the Hanson brothers would have been bundles of nerves in the days leading up to the historic performance. However, a year of seasoning and confidence building left them cool as cucumbers. "We're not nervous at all," Zac declared. "We can't wait to get out and do it!" And do it they did. Hanson's performance brought the crowd to its feet and had everyone MMMBoppin' in the aisles!

The blond brothers did save up a tad of energy for their last live gig of the year. The following day, Hanson brought its brand of feel-good pop to Bean Town for a private show at the Avalon. The concert was broadcast on Boston's W-XKS.

MORE THAN MEETS THE EYE

At first look, Zachary may be the youngest and least experienced member of Hanson. You could also argue that because he's the shortest and at the back of the stage, behind the drum set, he's the least visible. In fact, many photographers have commented that it's difficult to see him at concerts. Anthony Cutajar, Roger Glazer, and Ernie Paniccioli, three photographers who've provided fans with many color pinups by following Hanson in concert over the past year, all found it very challenging to shoot Zac during the group's performance at the U.S. Open last August. This is why good close-up shots of Zac are sometimes harder to come by than ones of Taylor or Isaac.

THE LIFE OF THE PARTY

Regardless of his age, height, or inexperience, Zac is an invaluable member of Hanson. He is an integral part of the group's live show, and not just because he maintains the beat. Zac's boundless energy plays a big part in getting the crowd fired up during a Hanson performance. When Hanson filmed the live part of the *Tulsa, Tokyo, and the Middle of Nowhere* video at New York City's Beacon Theater, it was Zac who got the crowd going. With fifteen thousand eager fans chanting, "We want Hanson!" Zac came running out onto the stage shooting Silly String into the crowd! During *Meet Hanson,* the ABC special, Zac got the only screams out of the calm, small audience by pretending he was going to leap into the crowd.

Before a Halloween promotional concert for Chicago's B-96 FM, fans waited outside by the dressing-room entrance, hoping to catch a glimpse of Hanson. As they shouted, "We want Hanson!" Zac stepped out and responded, "You want me?" with a smile and then ran back inside. Ike, Tay, and Zac wondered how they would hold their own against the likes of Backstreet Boys and Robyn, who also performed at the sold-out Rosemont Horizon arena that night. The crowd immediately showed its enthusiasm for the brothers when Zac came onstage dressed like a motorcycle racer!

Even from the outset, when Zac was nine and then ten, and Hanson was performing in front of small crowds at local school auditoriums, Zac's role in the band was becoming evident. Taylor recalls, "When we gave out T-shirts onstage, there was this one girl who reached out her hand, but she was too shy. Zac went into the crowd and picked her up and carried her onto the stage!"

COMIC RELIEF

Zac also provides much-needed comic relief for the Hanson brothers when they are on the road. You may think that with the serious nature of establishing a music career at their ages, there's no place for goofing around. On the contrary! Ike, Tay, and Zac are still young kids at heart who miss their friends, family, and home back in Tulsa. They get nervous when they do things for the first time, whether it's performing their first live show, recording their first album, shooting their first video, or going to a new foreign country. They also get frustrated trying to write songs together while they are all still improving on their respective instruments. This is where Zac, the court jester, comes into play. One funny remark or silly stunt on his part, and Ike and Tay forget their problems and laugh out loud with him. Before long, they remember why they formed a band in the first place: to have fun!

The first time the Hansons got together with the Dust Brothers, they were reminded of the importance of having a good time. The producing duo invited Hanson to their studio to record a few songs and after a while suggested they take a break and go for a swim. As mentioned before, at one point Zac jumped into the pool fully clothed. For the second song, he played the drums soaking wet!

Before their performance at the U.S. Open Tennis Center last summer, Isaac and Taylor appeared a bit nervous during Hanson's center-court interview with MTV, *Entertainment Tonight,* and *USA Today.* Zac lightened things up, however, first by pretending a tennis racket was a guitar and then by pretending to smash Taylor over the head with it and making the appropriate sound effects.

Don't think for a minute, however, that Zac is all fun, games, and nonsense. When it comes time to get things done, he's all business. Take Hanson's interview with *Entertainment Weekly,* for example. When the writer changed the subject to religion, something the

Hanson brothers and their family consider very personal, Zac cut them off, saying, "What we're focused on is the music and this album, *Middle of Nowhere.*"

NOT JUST SNARES AND CYMBALS

Zac brings a lot more to Hanson than just his drumsticks. For one thing, he never goes on-stage without his mini-maraca (that black ball he shakes during acoustic sets is full of beads) and a megaphone. He's also a songwriter and a singer. Don't call him a backup singer, either! Zac sings lead on "Lucy," "Man from Milwaukee," and the *Snowed In* cover songs "What Christmas Means to Me" and "Rockin' Around the Christmas Tree."

While most Hanson songs were cowritten by the brothers together with Mark Hudson, Zac played a bigger role in "Lucy." Hudson says, "I wanted to write a song with each brother. 'Lucy' was Zac's. I helped with the lyrics but kept his perspective."

"The day that I left Lucy, a tear fell from her eye. Now I don't have nobody, and I was such a fool . . ."

Not bad for a kid! But is this tale of heartbreak based on real events in Zac's life? Hardly. As Hudson puts it, "There's a signed lithograph of the Schroeder and Lucy characters from the *Peanuts* cartoon strip in my studio. I was looking at it when the boys were there and suddenly pictured Zac's face instead of Schroeder's."

There's a little more to it than that, though. As Zac explains it, "You know how Schroeder's like, 'Lucy, get off of me'? I'm doing the part of Schroeder. And how he's saying, 'Lucy, get off my back,' and he regrets it, and in the end, he really liked her."

If you've ever read through the liner notes of *Middle of Nowhere,* you probably noticed that the writing of each song is credited to all three band members equally. "Everybody contributes everything," Isaac declares. "It never happens that any one of us has more input than another. Generally, someone will start a song, and everyone else will chime in."

"It either works that way, or we'll all sit down together and write the whole song. It's just based on who has the best idea," Zac adds.

So where does someone so young get the inspiration to write music? "Inspiration comes from everyday life," Zac confirms. "Sometimes you can look out the window and something happens that'll inspire a song."

Take, for example, "Man from Milwaukee," a bonus track only included on the CD version of *Middle of Nowhere.* Zachary not only sings lead on this one, but the idea and the lyrics are entirely based on an experience in his life. "I was in Albuquerque with my family when our van broke down," he explains. "I was sitting at a bus stop waiting for my parents to fix it, when this guy sat down next to me. I'd been thinking about aliens, and I suddenly thought, 'What if he's really an alien?' So I started writing this song. Only Albuquerque didn't have the right ring to it, so I changed it to Milwaukee."

A few more tidbits add to the fun of "Man from Milwaukee." First, when Hanson performs the song live, Zac trades in his drum set for a megaphone to create alien voice effects. Second, the name of Hanson's debut album is taken from this song. "'Milwaukee' is about a guy at a bus stop in the middle of nowhere, and we thought that sounded kind of cool," Zac explains. Last, one of the lyrics in the song is "I think he's wacky." When Zac sings this line, he's most likely referring to the alien, but he could just as easily be singing about himself.

THE SKY'S THE LIMIT

When asked about his future, Zac kids, "I'd rather not think that far ahead. I've got a lot of time ahead of me." Who could blame him? He's got enough on his mind right now. But, as fans, we must ponder the possibilities. After all, at twelve, almost fifteen, and seventeen, the Hanson brothers can only get better as musicians, songwriters, and performers.

One thing's for sure, Hanson is here to stay. When the brothers signed to Mercury Records, their contract called for six albums. *Middle of Nowhere* and *Snowed In* make two, so look for at least four more great CDs from the blond trio over the next few years. Expect plenty of touring as well. As the band writes more material and grows more seasoned with

82

each performance, you can bet it'll soon be selling out big outdoor stadiums just like their idols Aerosmith have been doing for years.

MTV recently asked Hanson, "With so much success so early, what's left for Hanson to strive for?"

"There's a lot to strive for!" Zac responded.

"We've just barely started," Taylor added. "There are so many places to go, so much time to expand."

"And so many more instruments to learn!" Zac piped in. "You want to learn anything you can."

What about plans for expanding the band or starting a second, younger Hanson group? Hey, with so many siblings in a musical family, anything's possible. Zac kids about his three-year-old brother, Mackenzie, continuing the legacy. "Mackie's got the rhythm. I've got to watch out, or he'll steal my place."

OUTSIDE PROJECTS

There's also more to life than music, right? Rumors on the Internet have included a Saturday-morning Hanson cartoon like the Jackson Five used to have or a line of dolls modeled after the brothers, but Hanson denies it and would never want to be a part of anything "cheesy." All hope to see more of the Hanson brothers' beautiful mugs is not lost, however. "I hope we get to stay in the music biz and maybe do some acting or directing films or something like that." Great idea, Zac!

A recent *People* magazine feature suggested the Hanson brothers might star in a *My Three Sons* type of movie. Cute idea, but it ain't happenin'. However, Hanson's agents at the William Morris Agency have been in talks for a movie based on their lives. Producer Galt Neiderhoffer has purchased the rights to the Hanson brothers' life story, and writer Morgan J. Freeman (no relation to the actor) has been signed on to create a script. Neiderhoffer and Freeman previously worked together on *Hurricane Streets,* an independent film that garnered substantial praise at last year's Sundance Film Festival. The movie featured teen actor Brendan Sexton III (who starred in *Welcome to the Dollhouse).*

Don't count on the Brothers H joining an ensemble cast and putting out a movie à la Madonna. Since such a movie would be based, at least loosely, on the lives of the Hanson brothers and the story behind their success and would star Isaac, Taylor, and Zachary as themselves, it would likely be more of a documentary like the Beatles' *A Hard Day's Night* or, more recently, U2's *Rattle & Hum*. However, since the Hanson brothers are all about high-energy fun, it could be closer to the recent Spice Girls movie, *Spice World*, except, of course, not quite as over the top! Do you suppose many Hanson fans would be interested in such a film? You bet!

Hanson has also been in discussions to develop their own TV sitcom. Since their ABC *American Bandstand* and *Saturday Night Live* appearances went so well, and since the trio is so charismatic, their agents at William Morris have been throwing around the idea of a Hanson TV show. Ike, Tay and Zac enthusiastically discussed the plans with *Entertainment Tonight*, but pointed out that nothing was definite. People close to the band have said that the show would be a cross between *The Monkees* and *The Larry Sanders Show*.

THE FAN FRENZY CONTINUES

With so much going on right now and so much fan mail continuing to pour in, there's no reason to believe that Hanson won't be just as big this year as they were last year. With dreamy faces to match their great music, TV stations and magazines will keep clamoring for Isaac, Taylor, and Zachary as much as the radio stations do. As for their fans, well, we'll just leave that part up to you.

Bands break up all the time. In the past few years alone, popular groups like Soundgarden, the Talking Heads, Ned's Atomic Dustbin, and 10,000 Maniacs have split up. Rumors also have swirled about Oasis, Stone Temple Pilots, and even the Spice Girls.

What about Hanson? "We can't break up. We're brothers!" Zac jokes. Even if Hanson-mania begins to fade? Yeah, right, like a meteor hits planet Earth and we all start acting backward—listening to crummy music and liking mean, ugly boys! Anyway, just in case, Zac has a backup plan. "Actually, I'd like to be a cartoonist if this doesn't work out. I don't want to be stuck behind a desk."

ARE YOU THE ONE FOR ZAC?

Although there are thousands of girls who'd love to date any one of the Hanson brothers, the guys' busy schedule doesn't allow for a whole lot of time for dating. As Zac explains it, "They'd see us about one minute a year!" Regardless, young Zac certainly has shown an interest in girls, and at some point his busy schedule has got to open up.

Zac has given a wild array of answers to the "Do you have a girlfriend?" question that teen magazines like to ask. His answers have ranged from "No, I don't have one!" to "Who knows? Maybe! I'm still looking!" to "You can't avoid getting girls if you're a guy in a band!" It may be too early on in his life, and in this stage of his band's career, for Zac to consider a girlfriend, but he obviously has a soft spot for girls.

So, what kind of girl is the right one for Zac? Well, for one thing, she'd have to have the patience of a saint. Dating a celebrity isn't as glamorous as it may seem. Sure, you'd get to travel sometimes, meet interesting people (including Isaac and Taylor!), and get to do exciting things (such as seeing all of Hanson's performances from the front row), but you'd also have to go weeks or months at a time without seeing your boyfriend! Not to mention the fact that there'd be plenty of times when you'd be itching to see the new Leonardo DiCaprio movie while Zac needs to practice his new drum solo!

Other than patience, you'd certainly need a sense of humor so you could laugh along with Zac, a high energy level so you could keep up with him, and, of course, a love of music so you could keep on listening to his band's new music. That's the easy part, however. Obviously, Zac could never date the jealous type. With so many girls sending him fan mail and screaming his name, a jealous girlfriend would likely pull all her hair out in frustration! Other personality traits Zac might list if he were posting a personal ad are encouraging, fun-loving, active, and adventurous.

What type of boyfriend would he make?

Zac's a Libra, which means he's charming, amiable, and emotional and appreciates beauty, luxury, and all the good things life has to offer. Love and companionship are extremely important to Libras. One interesting trait of Libras is that they are often described as mediators. This means they seek and resolve differences between opposed sides to restore peace. (No wonder Ike and Tay never argue!) Libras are also among the more creative people. Their ruling planet is Venus, which means they have a genuine love of beauty and often possess artistic and creative talents. Since Zac enjoys drawing and cartooning as much as he does playing music, he's certainly no exception to this rule.

One trait that definitely suits Zac to a tee is that Libras are likely to seek attention. As you know, Zachary Hanson can never get enough applause from the crowd, screams from the fans, or laughs from his brothers. As a Libra, Zac is as likely to be creative and imaginative in his personal life as he is in his professional life. Simply put, he's a romantic at heart. Don't expect flowers on Valentine's Day. A Libra is likely to do something more creative that would really knock your socks off, such as writing you a personalized poem or song and then treating you to a fun day of all the activities you love the most!

When asked by a teen magazine to describe his perfect date, Zac replied, "I don't know. There are a lot . . . out there!" He's certainly got a sense of humor about dating. Zac's time will come, and when it does, there will be no shortage of willing girls waiting in the wings.

NUMEROLOGY

Most Hanson fanatics probably think Zac is the number one drummer in the world. And on the cutie scale, he rates a perfect ten. But in numerology terms, he's a seven. Numerology is an age-old method of determining someone's personality type that was originally developed by ancient Babylonians. The method calls for assigning each person a number from one through nine, determined by the letters in his or her full name (middle names are included). It's a pretty easy way to figure out what type you are. It also works for best friends, school crushes, and favorite celebrities. After testing the method on Zac, it was determined that he was a seven.

Here's how to do it. First, you write out

91

Zachary's full name (yes, spelling does count here) and then match the letters up with the following chart.

1	2	3	4	5	6	7	8	9
A	B	C	D	E	F	G	H	I
J	K	L	M	N	O	P	Q	R
S	T	U	V	W	X	Y	Z	

ZACHARY WALKER HANSON
8 1 3 8 1 9 7 5 1 3 2 5 9 8 1 5 1 6 5

The next step is to add up all of the corresponding numbers. In Zac's case, if you've been doing your math homework, you should come up with 88. The last step in this simple formula is to add the two numbers together until you get a single digit. In this example, 8 + 8 = 16, and then 1 + 6 = 7. This makes Zac a lucky 7. By the way, Zac's a math whiz himself, so don't think he couldn't have done this himself!

So, what are we saying about Zac here? In numerology, a personality type seven is an original person who is full of new and exciting ideas. Typically, sevens are deep thinkers who love to get extra-involved in their projects. Sevens feel as if once they set their minds to something, they must do the best job they possibly can. If this means putting in long hours or making sacrifices, then so be it! Sevens set the highest possible standards for themselves in every aspect of their lives. They are truly perfectionists. Sevens are often shy people (at least inwardly, in Zac's case!). Sevens are very compatible with nines, fours, sevens, and eights.

Are you compatible with Zachary? Do your numbers add up? Figure it out. Here are descriptions of the traits for the other numbers.

Ones are natural leaders. They always keep organized but tend to take on too much work themselves. Ones crave attention, but they should share it once in a while because others sometimes find ones to be a bit selfish. But not everyone. After all, everybody needs friends. That's where numbers two and six come in!

The most reserved and quiet of all the numbers is two. However, **twos** are talkative around those they know best, and because of that, they make great companions. Twos usually aren't too quick to judge others or a situation before knowing all the details. On the down side, twos tend to be a bit oversensitive at times, and they don't take to constructive criticism very well. Nonetheless, there are plenty of sevens, eights, and other twos out there for them to hang out with.

Threes are rather complex. On the one hand, they can make themselves at home anywhere they go and can easily make themselves the life of the party. They are usually quite charming as well. On the other hand, they tend to be a little bossy and domineering. Besides fours and fives, threes don't get along too well with others.

Fours are tremendous people who are responsible and serious yet also interesting and funny. They make great friends, too. What's not to like? Typical fours have a problem with putting their feet in their mouths a little too often. But that never seems to bother twos, threes, and eights. Fours' very best friends are usually fives and sixes.

Always looking for something more exciting? You must be a five. Outgoing, energetic, and adventurous are the best way to describe **fives**. Sounds like a great formula for success, except that fives tend to be spendthrifts. Fives are compatible with threes, sevens, and twos.

* * *

Sixes are naive people who tend to get taken for a ride. They also have a rep for putting their noses where they don't belong. On the bright side, however, a six is usually kind and generous. Ones, eights, and nines all appreciate that.

If your number is seven, look back at the numerology traits listed for Zac. **Sevens** like you and Animal are two peas in a pod!

Eights make good friends but also good enemies. If your best pal's an eight, she'll likely bring you all the assignments you missed when you were out sick. On the flip side, if you've got any eights for enemies, guess who talked behind your back that day? Eights are also hard workers and born leaders. Eights match up well with twos, fours, sixes, sevens, and nines.

Nines are good-hearted people, in the broad sense. In other words, nines might go to great lengths to save the rain forest or pitch in at an animal shelter but at the same time forget that their best friends really need them. Nines tend to ride an emotional roller coaster, with their strong feelings constantly fluctuating with their surroundings. Fours, sevens, and eights all make good pals for nines.

ZAC FACTS

Full name: Zachary Walker Hanson.
Nicknames: Zac, Animal.
Instruments: Drums, vocals, mini-maraca, megaphone.
Birthdate: October 22, 1985.
Birthplace: Tulsa, Oklahoma.
Hometown: Tulsa, Oklahoma.
Parents: Walker and Diana.
Siblings: Isaac, Taylor, Jessica, Avery, Mackenzie, and one on the way.
Hair color: Blond.
Eye color: Brown.
Height: 5'3".
Weight: Less than 100 pounds.
Shoe size: 8.

96

Zodiac sign: Libra.

Numerology trait number: 7.

Favorites

Color: Blue.

Musicians: Boyz II Men, En Vogue, Aerosmith.

Sports: Soccer, Rollerblading, skateboarding.

Food: Rex's Boneless Chicken in Tulsa, McDonald's, pepperoni pizza.

Dessert: Jell-O, chocolate ice cream.

Fashion staple: Colored Doc Martens boots.

Hobbies: Laser Quest, drawing, Sega, Nintendo 64, Sony PlayStation.

Movies: Action movies like *Total Recall* and *Twister*.

TV show: *Animaniacs*.

School subject: Math.

Hidden talents: Making comic books, and, according to a Web posting, can speak while belching!

Unusual hobby: Collects miniature shampoo bottles from hotels around the world.

Most embarrassing moment: Once fell backward off his seat in the middle of a drum solo.

Little-known facts: Zac's left-handed, his mom

braids his hair for him, and he may be getting braces soon.

Telling quote: "I always have to be wacky. When I act serious, it's like, 'Why aren't you wacky? Is this a bad day for you?'"

FAN MAIL INFO

There are a number of ways in which to send your love to Zac and his bros. On the Internet, there are more sites and links than you can keep up with, and there are also four addresses where you can send your warm regards the old-fashioned way. A few things to keep in mind:

(1) If you're surfing the Net in search of Hanson gossip, don't believe everything you hear. After all, you don't have to be an authority on Hanson to post materials about the group on the Internet. In fact, anybody with the right equipment and a little know-how can fire up a Web site.

(2) When you send regular mail, you might want to use a little creativity so that your fan

99

letter stands out from the millions of others. A few suggestions? If you're addressing one particular band member, use an envelope in his favorite color (Zac's is blue). Hanson, Zac and Tay especially, are way into drawing and cartooning, so if you've got some artistic talent, spice up your letter with a sketch or two. And don't forget birthdays. It may sound trite, but the guys are on the road so much that when their birthdays roll around, they usually don't get to cut a cake with the family or have fun with their friends. A well-timed birthday card from a fan could really make them smile, not to mention pick up a pen and respond to your letter!

(3) Don't get upset if you don't hear back from Hanson right away. There aren't too many people in the entire world who are as busy as this trio. Traveling, practicing, performing, and school don't leave much time for anything other than rest. Hanson will respond to fan mail, but it may take a while.

(4) Don't expect a personalized letter. Zac and his brothers get close to a million fan letters a month, according to one magazine editor's estimate. That doesn't include how many e-mails or Web site hits they get on top of that. Hanson appreciates its fans, but nobody (not even a super-talented trio) can pos-

sibly have the time to sit down and handwrite thousands of responses per week.

(5) Get your parents' permission before calling the Hanson Phone Hotline. It's long-distance.

Official fan club: Hanson Fan Club
c/o Hitz List
P.O. Box 703136
Tulsa, OK 74170

Record company: Hanson
c/o Mercury Records
11150 Santa Monica Blvd.,
suite 1100
Los Angeles, CA 90025

c/o Mercury Records
825 Eighth Ave.
New York, NY 10019

Management: Hanson
c/o Triune Music Group
8322 Livingston Way
Los Angeles, CA 90046

*Official Hanson
phone hotline:*   (918) 446-3979

*Official Internet
Web sites:*   http://www.hansonline.com
http://www.hansonhitz.com

Fan club e-mail: http://hansonfans
@hansonline.com

Mercury Records: http://www.polygram.com/
mercury/artists/hanson

Links to other sites: http://members.aol.com.
Crescent14/hlink.html

Hanson fact sheet: http://members.aol.com/G
Squiggles/hansonfacts.html

Once you've got the right resources, all you need to get a response is persistence and a little patience. Good luck, and stay tuned!

TEST YOUR ZAC KNOWLEDGE

After reading this book, you should be a certified expert on all things Zac. Over the past year, you've probably spent more time reading up on Zac and his brothers than you have spent doing your history homework. Think of the grades you'd get if history were as interesting as Hanson is to read about! You and your classmates are always arguing in the school hallways about Hanson facts and who is truly their number one fan. Let's see how much you really know. After you take this test, check the answers starting on page 107 (remember, no cheating!). Then turn to page 110 to see how you measure up.

103

1. How many siblings does Zac have?
2. What are their names?
3. Which one did Zac jokingly say might take his place behind the drum set one day?
4. What are Zac's parents' names?
5. What grade is Zac in?
6. When is Zac's birthday?
7. What does that make his zodiac sign?
8. What nickname did Isaac and Taylor give Zac?
9. What are Zac's favorite fashion staples?
10. Where is Zac's favorite place to go in Tulsa?
11. How old was Zac when he and his brothers first got serious about music?
12. True or false: Zac watches a lot of TV.
13. On what two songs on *Middle of Nowhere* does Zac sing lead?
14. Where was Hanson when Zac pretended a tennis racket was a guitar?
15. True or false: Zac is dating a young actress.
16. When Hanson appeared on *FOX After Breakfast*, what guest actress did Zac fling doughnuts at?
17. Why are good close-up performance pictures of Zac harder to come by than ones of Ike and Tay?

18. When Hanson performed at the mall in Paramus, New Jersey, only a few hundred people were expected to attend. How many actually showed up?

19. In what city did Hanson perform a special Halloween concert where Zac dressed up in costume?

20. How many songs on *Snowed In* are original Hanson compositions?

21. Which songs on *Snowed In* does Zac sing lead on?

22. Although dad Walker was a guitar player, what does he do for a living?

23. What countries did the Hanson family have to relocate to because of Dad's job?

24. At what fair did Hanson first perform on the community stage?

25. In what city did Hanson film the video for "Where's the Love"?

26. Where did the Hanson brothers make their very first performance, an unrehearsed, a cappella singing of do-wop songs?

27. Some live footage for *Tulsa, Tokyo, and the Middle of Nowhere,* as well as the MTV video for "I Will Come to You," were both filmed during a special performance. Where did this event occur?

28. Where was Hanson when the group was

unable to receive a special award from the governor of Oklahoma?

29. Where did Zac get his first set of drums?
30. Where did the idea for the song "Lucy" come from?
31. Where did Zac jump into a pool with all his clothes on?
32. What were the names of Hanson's two earlier independent albums?
33. What is the name of Hanson's manager?
34. What Mercury Records executive signed them to their contract?
35. What name has Zac given to Hanson fans who make lots of noise at shows and appearances?
36. In what city did Hanson perform with many other bands as part of a two-day charity festival?
37. True or false: Zac likes to eat at a Tulsa restaurant called Rex's Boneless Chicken.
38. Who tutors Zac and his brothers when they are on the road?
39. Besides drums, what instrument does Zac sometimes play?
40. What prop does he sometimes bring with him onstage?
41. What color are Zac's eyes?
42. True or false: Zac once pulled a fan onstage.

43. What is the song "Yearbook" about?
44. When did Zac drive a crowd crazy by pretending to jump over a railing?
45. What fun things are in Zac's backyard at home?
46. What is Zac's favorite color?
47. Who helped Hanson write the song "Weird"?
48. Who is the only musician to record a number one hit at a younger age than Zac?
49. What is Zac's favorite song on *Middle of Nowhere?*
50. Whom did Hanson dedicate its Christmas album, *Snowed In,* to?

ANSWERS TO THE ZAC KNOWLEDGE TEST

1. Six. Zac has two older brothers, obviously, two younger sisters, a younger brother, and a brand new baby sib on the way!
2. Isaac, Taylor, Jessica, Avery, and Mackenzie (plus one on the way).
3. His three-year-old brother, Mackenzie.
4. Walker and Diana.
5. The equivalent of sixth grade in homeschool.
6. October 22, 1985.

7. Libra.
8. Animal, after the zany Muppets character who also plays the drums.
9. His Doc Martens shoes.
10. Laser Quest.
11. He was only six years old.
12. False. He doesn't have much time for TV, and besides, he's more of an outdoors kind of guy.
13. "Lucy" and "Man from Milwaukee."
14. They were performing a concert at Arthur Ashe Day in Queens, New York.
15. False! Zac doesn't even have a girlfriend, so there's hope for you yet!
16. *Suddenly Susan*'s Kathy Griffin.
17. Because Zac is short and often can't be seen clearly from behind the drum set.
18. Six thousand!
19. Chicago, Illinois.
20. Three. "At Christmas," "Christmas Time," and "Everybody Knows the Claus."
21. "What Christmas Means to Me," "Rockin' Around the Christmas Tree," and parts of "Silent Night Medley."
22. He's an executive for an oil company in Tulsa.
23. Ecuador, Venezuela, and Trinidad.
24. Tulsa's Mayfest.

25. London, England.
26. At a family Christmas party at Walker's company.
27. At the Beacon Theater in New York City.
28. In New York, taping their segment for *The Late Show with David Letterman*.
29. A friend's attic.
30. A *Peanuts* cartoon strip lithograph on the wall in co-songwriter Mark Hudson's office.
31. At the Dust Brothers' house.
32. *Boomerang* and *MMMBop*.
33. Christopher Sabec.
34. Steve Greenberg.
35. The "Scream Squad."
36. In Miami, Florida, for the annual Y-100 Wing Ding event.
37. True. It's Zac's favorite restaurant.
38. Mom, Diana.
39. Mini-maraca.
40. A megaphone.
41. Brown.
42. True. During an early show at a school gymnasium, a young girl was too shy to come onstage to get a free T-shirt, so Zac carried her up!
43. A missing classmate.
44. In Los Angeles, during Hanson's performance outside Sam Goody at Universal City Walk.

45. A soccer goal and a treehouse that the family built themselves.
46. Blue.
47. Desmond Child.
48. Michael Jackson was one month younger.
49. He doesn't have a favorite. He likes them all.
50. Their fans.

SCORING

Tally up your score, and see how big a Zac fan you are!

38–50 correct: Nice job! You probably know as much about Zac as his brothers Ike and Tay do!

25–37 correct: Pretty good. You're definitely down with the Zac facts!

15–24 correct: Not bad. You might know a thing or two about Zac, but not enough to be a major fanatic. Maybe you're more into Taylor and Isaac? (Not that that's a bad thing. They're red-hot rockers themselves, too!)

10–14 correct: You've got some Hanson homework to do. Better start stocking up on teen mags and spending some more time on-line.

0-9 correct: Put this book back where you found it! Your sister will be so upset if she can't find it later that she might just braid your hair to make *you* look like Zac!

ABOUT THE AUTHOR

Matt Netter is a freelance writer living and working in New York City.